pond circle

also by betsy franco

BEES, SNAILS, & PEACOCK TAILS

BIRDSONGS

COUNTING OUR WAY TO THE 100TH DAY!

MATHEMATICKLES!

SUMMER BEAT

Margaret K. McElderry Books

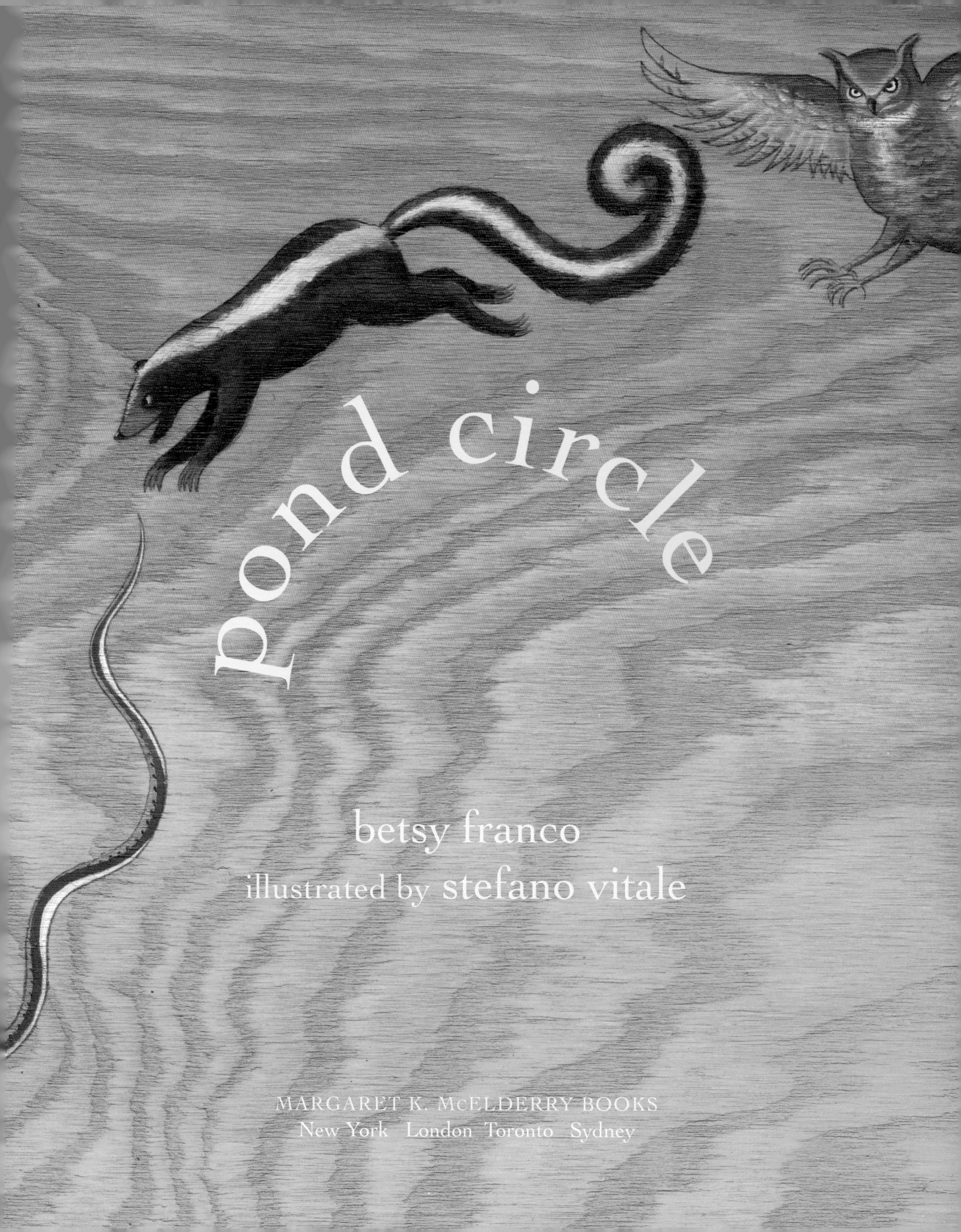

pond circle

betsy franco

illustrated by stefano vitale

MARGARET K. McELDERRY BOOKS

New York London Toronto Sydney

Thank you to Michael Elsohn Ross
and Lynn M. Hansen for their expert advice. — B. F.

Margaret K. McElderry Books
An imprint of Simon & Schuster Children's Publishing Division
1230 Avenue of the Americas, New York, New York 10020
Text copyright © 2009 by Betsy Franco
Illustrations copyright © 2009 by Stefano Vitale
Book design by Debra Sfetsios
The text for this book is set in Cochin.
The illustrations for this book are rendered in oil on wood.
Manufactured in China
4 6 8 10 9 7 5 3
Library of Congress Cataloging-in-Publication Data
Franco, Betsy.
Pond circle / Betsy Franco. — 1st ed.
p. cm.
Summary: In the pond by Anna's house, a food chain begins with algae,
which is eaten by a mayfly nymph, which is eaten by a beetle,
which is eaten by a bullfrog. . . .
ISBN: 978-1-4169-4021-0
[1. Food chains (Ecology) 2. Pond ecology — Fiction.
3. Ecology — Fiction. 4. Animals — Food — Fiction.] I. Title.
PZ7.F8475Po 2009
[E] — dc22
2008016268
1109 SCP

For James—B. F. To Ruben—S. V.

This is the water

    the deep, still water

that filled the pond

by Anna's house.

This is the algae

the jade green algae

that grew in the water

that filled the pond

by Anna's house.

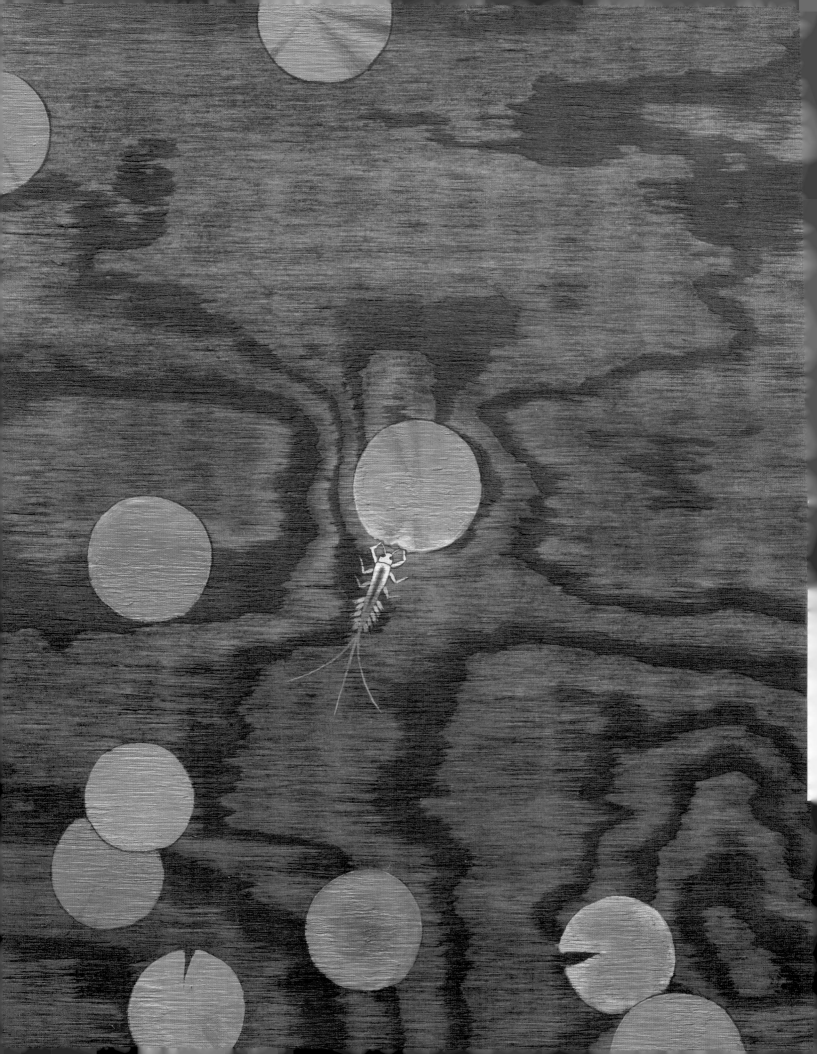

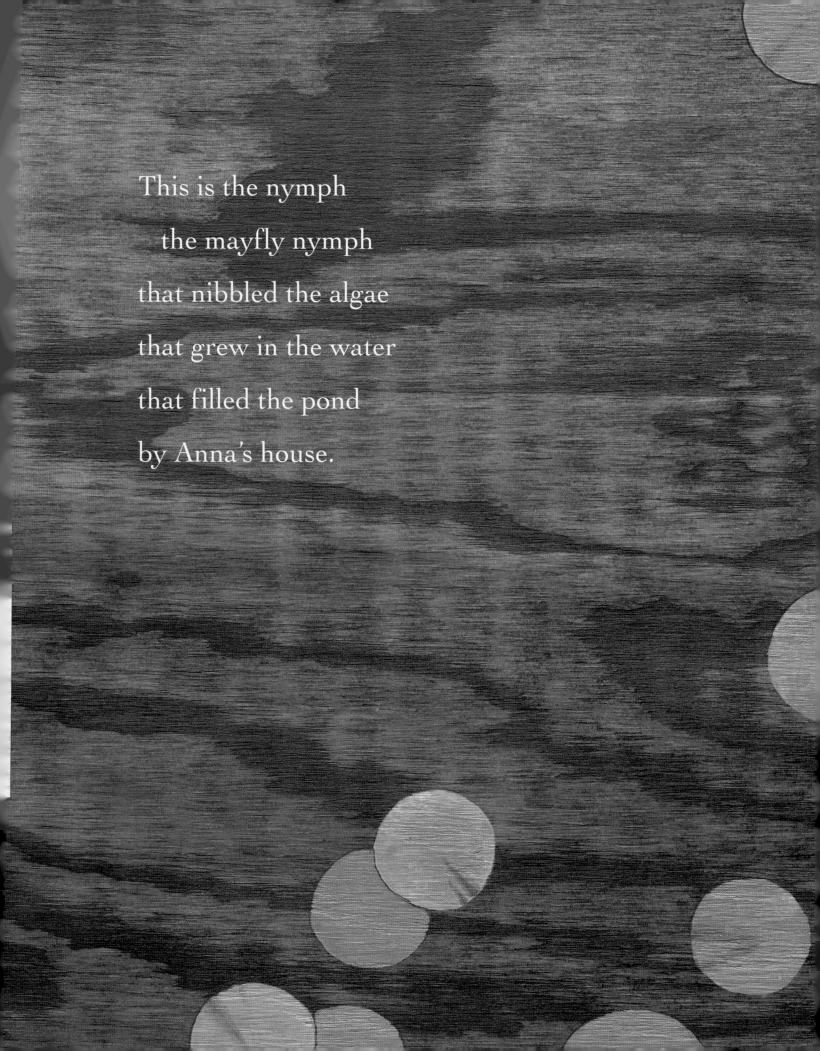

This is the nymph

   the mayfly nymph

that nibbled the algae

that grew in the water

that filled the pond

by Anna's house.

This is the beetle

the diving beetle

that ate the nymph

that nibbled the algae

that grew in the water

that filled the pond

by Anna's house.

This is the frog

the loud bullfrog

that gobbled the beetle

that ate the nymph

that nibbled the algae

that grew in the water

that filled the pond

by Anna's house.

This is the snake

the garter snake

that swallowed the frog

that gobbled the beetle

that ate the nymph

that nibbled the algae

that grew in the water

that filled the pond

by Anna's house.

This is the skunk

the shy striped skunk

that caught the snake

that swallowed the frog

that gobbled the beetle

that ate the nymph

that nibbled the algae

that grew in the water

that filled the pond

by Anna's house.

This is the owl

   the great horned owl

that dived for the skunk

that caught the snake

that swallowed the frog

that gobbled the beetle

that ate the nymph

that nibbled the algae

that grew in the water

that filled the pond

by Anna's house.

This is the raccoon

the hungry raccoon

that stole the eggs

of the great horned owl

that dived for the skunk

that caught the snake

that swallowed the frog

that gobbled the beetle

that ate the nymph

that nibbled the algae

that grew in the water

that filled the pond

by Anna's house.

This is the coyote

out in the dark

that stalked the raccoon

the hungry raccoon

that stole the eggs

of the great horned owl

that dived for the skunk

the shy striped skunk

that caught the snake

the garter snake

that swallowed the frog

the loud bullfrog

that gobbled the beetle

the diving beetle

that ate the nymph

the mayfly nymph

that nibbled the algae

the jade green algae

that grew in the water

the deep, still water

that filled the pond

by Anna's house.

I am the girl

   whose name is Anna

who heard the coyote

one summer night

by the deep, still water

where algae grows

mayflies dart

beetles dive

frogs spring

snakes swim

skunks shuffle

owls swoop

raccoons rummage

and coyotes howl.

I am the girl

who heard the coyote

looked up from her book

leaned out the window

and howled back

"Hello, hello,

hello, out there,"

across the darkness

and out to the pond

of deep, still water

by my house.

facts to
pond-er

Algae

Green algae are tiny plants that grow and float freely in ponds. Algae come in different forms. Sometimes they look like scum on the top of the pond. Algae are very important because they are at the bottom of the food chain. They get energy from the sun and pass the energy on to whatever eats them.

Mayfly nymph

The nymph is one stage of the insect called the mayfly. In its lifetime the mayfly goes from an egg to a nymph to a dun to an adult mayfly. The nymph feeds on algae, but the mayfly doesn't eat. The adult finds a mate, lays eggs, and dies, all in one day.

Predaceous diving beetle

The diving beetle lives in water. When it swims, it uses its long back legs. The beetle is known for its big appetite. When diving, it can carry air under its wings so that it can stay under for long periods of time.

Bullfrog

A bullfrog's croak is unforgettable. When the bullfrog was brought into the ponds of the Central Valley of California, it started eating the frogs that were living there. One of the native frogs, the California red-legged frog, is now a threatened species. It appeared in Mark Twain's story "The Celebrated Jumping Frog of Calaveras County."

Giant garter snake

The giant garter snake can swallow a frog bigger than its head by unlocking its jaws and swallowing the frog whole. It can be seen sunning itself and then dropping into the water. It is active both day and night. The giant garter snake is on the list of threatened animals.

Striped skunk

The striped skunk is a gentle, shy creature that hunts at night. It will eat almost anything, from insects to mice to turtle eggs. Snakes are a treat for a skunk. The striped skunk has a white V down its back and tail. It is bigger than the spotted skunk.

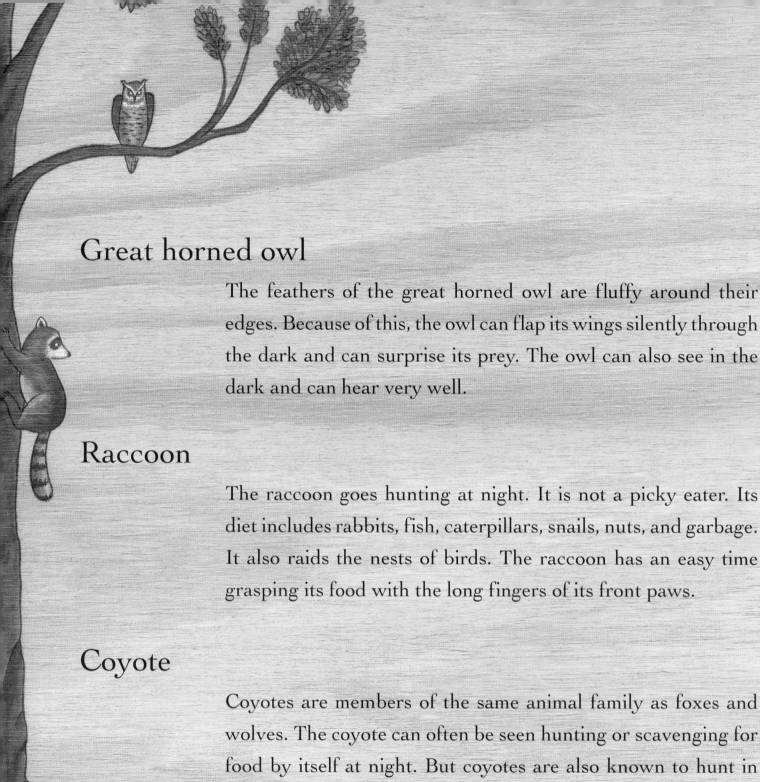

Great horned owl

The feathers of the great horned owl are fluffy around their edges. Because of this, the owl can flap its wings silently through the dark and can surprise its prey. The owl can also see in the dark and can hear very well.

Raccoon

The raccoon goes hunting at night. It is not a picky eater. Its diet includes rabbits, fish, caterpillars, snails, nuts, and garbage. It also raids the nests of birds. The raccoon has an easy time grasping its food with the long fingers of its front paws.

Coyote

Coyotes are members of the same animal family as foxes and wolves. The coyote can often be seen hunting or scavenging for food by itself at night. But coyotes are also known to hunt in pairs or in groups when they are stalking larger prey.